THE Black Sheep

Elisabeth Heck
Illustrated by Sita Jucker

Translated from the German
by Karen Klockner

Little, Brown and Company
Boston   Toronto

The shepherd should have been happy. All of his sheep followed him everywhere. All, that is, except one—the black sheep.

The shepherd worried about the black sheep. She always ran away from the rest of the flock and went off on her own.

One day, the time came for the shepherd
to shear his sheep. The sheep lined up one
by one, but as usual the black sheep ran
off alone. She wanted to keep her wool
for herself.

With a sigh, the shepherd called
his little boy and his dog. Together
they ran after the black sheep. But
suddenly she disappeared!

They searched and they searched, but couldn't find her. Where could that sheep have gone?

The black sheep was hiding all by herself in an empty cave she had discovered. She liked it there, where she could be alone and do anything she wanted all day long! Whenever she felt like it, she could run out and play in the open fields.

Soon autumn came. Then winter
storms began to blow, and the winds
were bitter and cold. The black sheep
shivered. She felt lonely and sad.

With the storms came the snow. It fell more and more heavily. The sheep couldn't even find her cave! She wandered around feeling very lost.

Suddenly, up ahead of her, she saw a glowing light. She started to walk towards it. The light was coming from her cave! Inside, it looked strangely bright. There she found a man and a woman who were taking shelter from the storm.

At first the black sheep wanted to run away. But then she saw a little child. The light seemed to surround him.

The woman picked up her baby to warm him. But the child began to cry.

The black sheep didn't run away. Her wool coat seemed heavy and warm. As she looked at the child, she felt even warmer inside. Slowly, she stepped closer and closer to the baby, and finally lay herself down next to him on the ground.

At first, the woman was very surprised. But after a moment she placed the child carefully in the sheep's warm wool. The baby stopped crying! The black sheep hardly dared to breathe.

Then, there was a sound at the entrance to the cave. They looked up and saw the shepherd. Behind him were all of his sheep.

When the shepherd saw the black sheep inside the cave, he said, "So! Here is my lost sheep at last! And she has saved her wool for this child. I will let her stay here and belong to him."

With those words, the shepherd gently lay his cloak over the child and the sheep.

Then he turned quietly and went on
his way. All of his sheep followed him,
and the shepherd felt happy at last.

Originally published in Switzerland under the title *Das Andere Schaf.*

Copyright © 1985 by bohem press, Zurich, Switzerland
English language translation Copyright © 1986 by Little, Brown and Company (Inc.)

Library of Congress Catalog Card No. 86-80171

First U.S. Edition

AHS
Printed in Italy